LEGO DISNEY PRINCESS

LOST *and* FOUND

Written by
Laura Buller

Illustrated by the
Ameet Studio Artists

D0019212

Copyright © 2018 Disney Enterprises, Inc. All rights reserved. Published by Disney Press, an imprint of Disney Book Group. No part of this book may be reproduced or transmitted in any form or by any means, electronic or mechanical, including photocopying, recording, or by any information storage and retrieval system, without written permission from the publisher. For information address Disney Press, 1200 Grand Central Avenue, Glendale, California 91201.

First Paperback Edition, October 2018
1 3 5 7 9 10 8 6 4 2
ISBN 978-1-368-02304-7
FAC-029261-18243
Library of Congress Control Number: 2018936732
Printed in the United States of America
For more Disney Press fun, visit www.disneybooks.com

SUSTAINABLE FORESTRY INITIATIVE
Certified Sourcing
www.sfiprogram.org
SFI-01415

CALGARY PUBLIC LIBRARY

DEC 2018

If you purchased this book without a cover, you should be aware that this book is stolen property. It was reported as "unsold and destroyed" to the publisher, and neither the author nor the publisher has received any payment for this "stripped" book.

There is a girl who loves to build with her LEGO bricks.

She built all the princess castles. Then she put them together. She made a big new castle. It is magical.

The girl loves the Disney Princesses, too. She put them in the castle. Now she makes up stories about them.

This is one of her stories. . . .

Welcome to the castle!
Say hello to all the princesses.

They play and have fun
together here.

Today is a busy day. But there is still time to play with the little puppy.

His paws are so muddy!

Princess Jasmine runs
into the room.

"Has anyone seen my gold vase? I can't find it!" she says.

The other princesses want
to help.

Mulan has an idea.
"We will help you!"

"Let's split up and look all over!" Mulan says.

The princesses cheer.
They will find the gold vase.

14

Ariel looks in her room.
She has lots of treasures there.
Aha!

Is that something shiny and
gold?

Ariel gives it a tug.
"It is the vase!" she shouts.

But Cinderella says, "That is a teapot, silly!"

Aurora looks in the forest.

She spots a sparkle
in the river.
Is it Jasmine's vase?

Aurora jumps into the water.
SPLASH!

The sparkly thing
swims away.
It was a goldfish!

Snow White is in
the flower garden.
She hopes her animal
friends can help her.

There are birds
and butterflies.
But what else will she find?

Snow White looks in the
flowers.
"I see something golden!"
she says.

Oh, no!
It is only a yellow watering can.

The princesses meet
in the flower garden.
Jasmine is sad.
No one has the vase.

But the princesses
do not give up.
"Come on, friends!" says
Rapunzel. "I have an idea!"

"We have looked high and low,"
says Rapunzel. "But we need
a better view."

Rapunzel explains her idea.
The friends get to work.

The princesses build stairs
up to the castle tower.
Wow! It is tall.

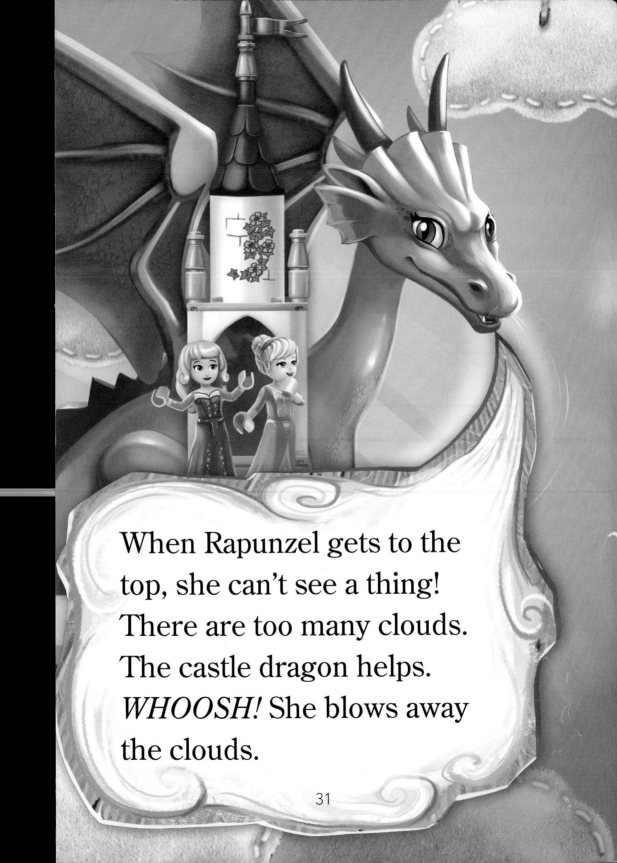

When Rapunzel gets to the top, she can't see a thing! There are too many clouds. The castle dragon helps. *WHOOSH!* She blows away the clouds.

"There it is!" says Rapunzel.
The vase is peeking out from
a pile of dirt. The puppy must
have hidden it!
"Oh, silly puppy!" Belle says.